128166

KU-664-548

**THE
TROUBLE
WITH
MR HARRIS**

First published 1978 by
André Deutsch Limited
105 Great Russell Street London WC1

Printed in Great Britain by
Sackville Press Billericay Ltd

British Library Cataloguing in Publication Data

Armitage, Ronda
  The trouble with Mr Harris.
  I. Title   II. Armitage, David
  823'.9'1J   PZ7.A/

  ISBN 0-233-96963-2

Copyright © 1978 by Ronda and David Armitage
All rights reserved

OXFORD
POLYTECHNIC
LIBRARY

To DOROTHY BUTLER

The Trouble With Mr Harris

Ronda and David Armitage

ANDRE
DEUTSCH

There was once a little village called Hodgeton.
It sat comfortably on the gentle slopes of the hills
beside the river Ince.

Three miles to the north west was the bustling town of Gutterville and two miles to the south east was the village of Derry Wole.

But the people of Hodgeton very rarely visited Gutterville
or Derry Wole as they found almost everything they
needed in their own village.
There was . . .

A Supermarket

A Butcher's Shop

A Draper's Shop

A Hardware Shop

A Chemist

A Baker's Shop

A Greengrocers

and a shop with a bit of everything

But the most important place in the village was the Post Office.

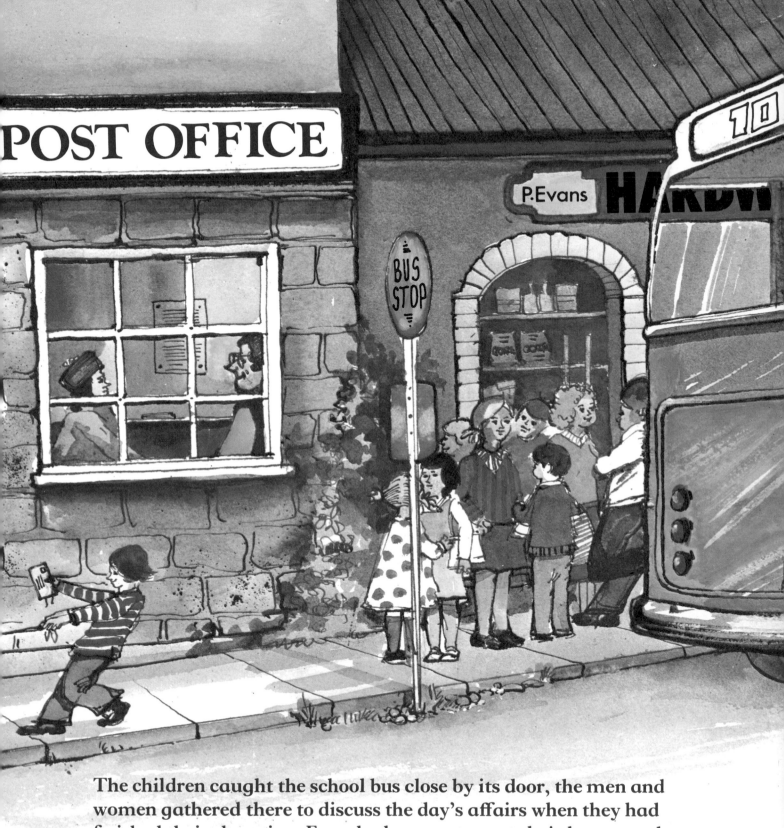

The children caught the school bus close by its door, the men and women gathered there to discuss the day's affairs when they had finished their shopping. Everybody came to post their letters and their parcels, but best of all they called to pass the time of day with the Postmaster. Or that was the way it used to be . . .

He came from **THE CENTRAL POST OFFICE** in Gutterville
and was used only to busy city ways where chatting and passing
the time of day were simply not allowed.

The people of Hodgeton were very surprised by their new Postmaster.

"Hurry along now," he snapped at old Mrs Bluett as she fumbled for her purse.

"The right money for the right stamps, please," he barked at Mr Hopkins the chemist.

"Tell your little boy that this is no place for drawing pictures," he said sternly to Mrs Fitch.

"That parcel will be in pieces before it gets half way to New Zealand," he warned Polly Plowden.

Indeed, the Post Office was no longer the same place. People wrapped their parcels with care, they gave the right money for the right stamps, and kept their children close beside them.

Nobody chatted, nobody laughed, and nobody passed the time of day with the Postmaster. In fact, one Friday his only visitor was a small girl called little Effie.

Instead, the people of Hodgeton caught the 9.15 bus to the village of Derry Wole where they bought their stamps, posted their letters and collected their pensions at the friendly Derry Wole Post Office. More often than not, while they were there, they bought their meat at the Derry Wole butchers, their toothpaste and soap at the Derry Wole chemist, their saucepans and spades at the Derry Wole hardware shop and their cakes and buns at the Derry Wole bakery. Finally, they caught the 12.15 bus back to Hodgeton.

The people of Hodgeton discussed their new Postmaster amongst themselves. "He's much too brusque," Mrs Reid complained to Mrs Dann the baker. "It's all post your parcels and out of the place."

"I used to look forward to my Post Office visits," sighed Captain McFooks, "but this new Postmaster, well, he's just not interested in talking to people. He's efficient, mind, but he just doesn't enjoy a good chat."

The disgruntled shopkeepers complained because people were shopping in Derry Wole. "What shall we do?" said Mr Hopkins the chemist.

"He'll have to go," said Peter Evans the hardware merchant.

So the shopkeepers decided to call a public meeting at the village hall to discuss the affair of Mr Harris.

PLEASE DO NOT PICK THE FLOWERS

VILLAGE HALL

NOTICES

PUBLIC
MEETING

THIS STONE WAS
LAID BY ROBERT
WITHERSPOON, MAYOR
OF HODGETON. 1911

It was an extremely noisy meeting. The mothers complained because Mr Harris frightened the children. The old people complained because he was so impatient and the shopkeepers complained because he was bad for business. "We want a happy, contented Postmaster in our Post Office," everyone agreed, "not a bad tempered, irascible man like Mr Harris."

"But he's not bad tempered and irascible," shouted little Effie from the back row. The people at the meeting looked most astonished.

"I beg your pardon, little Effie," queried Captain McFooks, "what makes you say that?"

"Because I know," said little Effie. "I've talked to him. He's never lived in a village before, he's lived only in large towns where people are always busy and in a hurry. He's not used to talking to people while he works, he's just a bit shy, that's all."

The people at the meeting looked even more astonished and just a trifle uncomfortable. They hadn't thought of how Mr Harris felt. They had been too concerned with their own affairs.

The next morning Mr Harris stood by himself at the doorway of the Post Office. It was a fine spring morning but it did not make Mr Harris feel particularly happy. Suddenly, a pram with little Effie's baby brother in it swept past. To Mr Harris's astonishment, nobody was holding the pram. In fact the pram was heading fast towards a busy side street.

Mr Harris practically flew out of the door scattering people in all directions.

"That man is always in such a hurry," said Miss Crabtree to Mrs Clarke.

Down the pavement he hurtled and with an almighty lunge, he caught the pram as it was about to run over the kerb and in front of a moving car.

Little Effie's mother was close behind. She grabbed little
Effie's baby brother and held him close. "Oh, Mr Harris,
thank you! Thank you! I am so glad that you moved so quickly—
I couldn't have got there in time."

"I am delighted that I could be of assistance,"
panted Mr Harris. The people of Hodgeton who
had seen what had happened crowded round and
patted Mr Harris on the back.

"By jove, that was quite a sprint,"
marvelled Mr Hopkins the chemist.

"Oh Mr Harris," quavered old
Mrs Bluett, dabbing at her
eyes with her handkerchief,
"you were just lovely."

KEEP
HODGETON
TIDY

Now the people of Hodgeton knew they had been wrong about Mr Harris. Captain McFooks and Mr Hopkins discussed the day's events as they strolled across to the pub that evening. "It was most fortunate that Mr Harris is so speedy and efficient," said Mr Hopkins, "he saved that baby's life today."

"I quite agree," said Captain McFooks. "I think little Effie was right. He is not used to village ways and we are not used to town ways. We must make amends."

So the people of Hodgeton decided to have a belated 'Welcome to Mr Harris' week. And this is how they did it . . . On Monday Mrs Bluett presented Mr Harris with a magnificent bunch of daffodils. He looked very surprised but thanked her politely.

On Tuesday Polly Plowden baked him a three-tiered chocolate sponge. "I hope you like chocolate," she enquired, a little anxiously.

"My *very* favourite cake," said Mr Harris.

On Wednesday, Elsie Bain, the butcher, arrived with a tasty sirloin of beef for him. She was sure he smiled as he thanked her.

It was cold in the Post Office on Thursday morning.
"My wife thought this hat and scarf might come in handy," said Captain McFooks, "she knitted it herself."
Mr Harris was delighted.

On Friday little Effie called to invite Mr Harris for Saturday tea. "I thought you might be lonely," she said, "so I brought Hector to keep you company." And Mr Harris smiled, a great, big enormous smile.

On Saturday morning Mr Harris chatted over the fence to Mr Hopkins the chemist. They discussed the possibility of planting early potatoes as the weather was so mild.

But Saturday's tea with little Effie and her family was the best part of the week. "I haven't eaten so well for many a day," said Mr Harris as he refused yet another piece of strawberry sponge.

So once again Hodgeton was a contented village. The people shopped at the local shops, posted their letters at the local Post Office and chatted with Mr Harris, their local Postmaster. The 9.15 bus to Derry Wole was almost always empty.

OXFORD
POLYTECHNIC
LIBRARY